Quick Smarts

SHARKS AND OTHER MONSTERS OF THE DEEP

Planet Water!

In some ways, we shouldn't call our planet "Planet Earth." It would be more accurate to call it "Planet Water." Why? Here are a few facts:

The oceans occupy almost 71% of our planet's surface and contain over 97% of all our planet's water.

The average depth of the ocean is over 2.5 miles (4 km).

The oceans provide 99% of the Earth's living space.

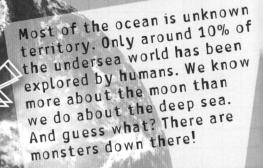

Most of the ocean is unknown territory. Only around 10% of the undersea world has been explored by humans. We know more about the moon than we do about the deep sea. And guess what? There are monsters down there!

The sunlight zone

0–660 ft (0–200 m)

Sunlight reaches this zone, filling it with lots of plants and animals.

The twilight zone

660–3,300 ft (200–1,000 m)

There's not much light here, so there are no plants. Sharks can be found here and in the sunlight zone.

The night zone

3,300–13,200 ft (1,000–4,000 m)

There's no light here. Sperm whales can swim this deep, but you are more likely to find strange creatures, like the anglerfish.

The deep sea & The deep-sea trench

3,300 ft (4,000 m) and below

The ocean depths are pitch black and icy cold. At certain points, the sea goes even lower into deep trenches. What creatures are waiting down there?

Ocean Layers

THE SUNLIGHT ZONE

THE TWILIGHT ZONE

THE NIGHT ZONE

THE DEEP SEA

THE DEEP-SEA TRENCH

The great white shark

With its huge, powerful, rocket-shaped body and rows of razor-sharp teeth, the great white shark is the scariest fish on the planet!

Using its **powerful** tail, a great white can swim up to **15 mph (24 kph)**!

White death

The great white shark is also known as the white pointer, the white shark, and the white death.

4

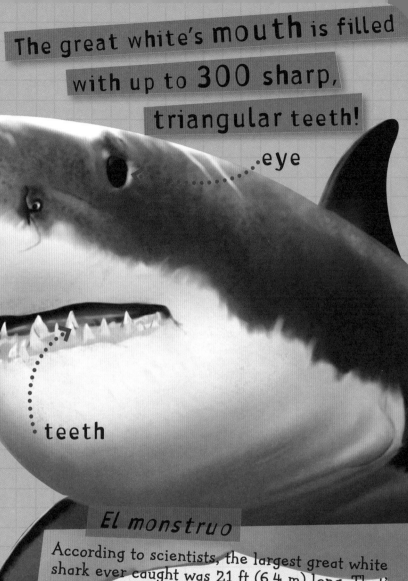

The great white's mouth is filled with up to 300 sharp, triangular teeth!

eye

teeth

El monstruo

According to scientists, the largest great white shark ever caught was 21 ft (6.4 m) long. That's over half the length of your school bus! It was known as, "*El Monstruo de Cojimar*," or "The Monster of Cojimar," after the fishing village in Cuba where it was caught in 1945.

Did you know?

The great white's teeth often break during attacks, but amazingly, other teeth will soon replace the broken ones. It can go through thousands of teeth in its lifetime!

The great white doesn't it swallows whole

Long-range hunter

Great whites can cover long distances. One great white was electronically tracked swimming from South Africa to the northwest coast of Australia and back—a journey of 12,400 miles (20,000 km)— in less than 9 months.

stop to chew its food— chunks instead!

Pup or prey?

A baby great white is called a pup. When a pup is born, it swims away from its mother and has to learn to fend for itself right away. Its own mother might even see it as prey for dinner!

Great whites have an acute sense of smell: they can detect the **scent of blood** up to 3 miles (5 km) away!

Shark attack!

There are three main types of shark attacks on humans. First, and most often, it's just a case of mistaken identity. Next, it might be an active attack for food or to defend its territory. And finally, in the worst case, the shark attacks to feed and will bite repeatedly.

fin

Mmm . . . sea lion

The great white shark's favorite food is not actually human beings, but seals and sea lions. It will also eat porpoises, seabirds, leopard sharks, penguins, and even the bodies of dead whales!

There are more shark attacks in Florida than anywhere else in the world!

Quick Smarts

Class: *Chondrichthyes*

Family: *Lamnidae*

Size: A typical adult is around 14–15 ft long (4.3–4.6 m), and weighs between 1,150–1,700 lb (522–771 kg). Females are usually larger than the males.

Lifespan: We don't really know. Estimates vary between 30 and 100 years!

Habitat: Coastal and offshore waters with a temperature between 54–75 °F (12–24 °C).

Weapons: Huge bodies, fast swimmers, powerful jaws and razor-sharp teeth. What more do you need?

Conservation: The great white is an endangered species. More sharks are killed each year by humans than the number of humans killed by sharks.

Q: Did you hear about the angry aquarium owner?

A: His shark was worse than his pike!

The moray eel

With two incredible sets of jaws and scary, sharp teeth, the moray eel could be straight out of a horror movie!

Is it a fish? Is it a snake?

The moray eel looks like a snake because its body is long, thick, and smooth, with only a few fins. Despite this, it's actually a scaleless fish!

Nosy, nosy

The moray has very poor eyesight, but a very good sense of smell. That's because it has TWO sets of nostrils: one at the front of the snout, the other above the eyes. That's like having eyebrows that can smell!

Lime slime

Most green moray eels actually have brown skin!
A thick yellow coat of mucus, or slime, on their body,
gives them the appearance of being green. Yuck!

The moray eel has over 130 vertebrae (sections of backbone), which makes it VERY flexible!

Moray eels can swim backwards as well as forwards and are very quick!

Moray eels seem **shy** but and unpredictable if you

Jaws two

As well as having two noses, the moray eel has two sets of jaws—an outer jaw and another set hidden down in its throat. The moray catches its prey with its outer jaws. Its hidden jaws then spring forward and grab the prey with curved, backward-pointing teeth that bite it to pieces and swallow it. It's the only known animal to do this!

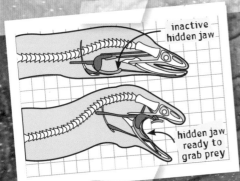

inactive hidden jaw

hidden jaw ready to grab prey

In a tight spot

Why do they need two jaws? Most fish suck up their food as if they're vacuums, expanding their heads to pick up food. Morays can't do this because they live in such tight spaces. No room for big heads!

can become **aggressive**
trespass on their patch!

sharp
teeth

Eel meal

All morays are carnivores, feeding on a
variety of fish, octopus, lobster, shrimp,
crabs—and even barnacles. A moray
only eats what it can swallow whole, so
the bigger the eel—the bigger the meal!

13

Reef encounter

Most moray eels live in rocky areas and hide in the smallest of openings. Divers often see them with their heads poking out of a hole in the reef! A few can also be found in muddy waters or estuaries.

Did you know?

Because most moray eels have so few fins, they have trouble staying upright for long. It is not uncommon to see them drifting on their sides, or even lying upside down!

Eel appeal

All eels have the potential to be both male and female. Some start as males and then later change to females. Other species have both male and female parts. How confusing!

Quick Smarts

Class: *Actinopterygii*

Family: *Muraenidae*

Size: The longest is the slender giant moray, measuring up to 13 ft (4 m). The white spotted dwarf moray is the smallest. It only grows to 7 in (18 cm).

Lifespan: Morays may live as long as 5-10 years, although some have lived to 30 years.

Habitat: Most species are found on coral reefs in fairly shallow, warm waters. They have been seen in the Caribbean, the Gulf of Mexico, parts of Asia, and off the East Coast in the US.

Weapons: A large mouth and two sets of deadly jaws!

Conservation: These eels are not considered endangered. In some countries they are caught for food—but some are poisonous and could cause serious sickness or even death!

Q: What does a moray use for power?

A: Eel-ectricity.

15

The stingray

Imagine you're as flat as a pancake, with eyes on the top of your body and a mouth and nose on your belly . . . now you know how a stingray feels!

Friendly or deadly?

Don't be fooled by the friendly appearance of the stingray. It has a large, poisonous spine in its tail and can be very dangerous! In some species this deadly weapon grows to over 12 in (30 cm) long.

Hide-and-seek

The stingray's appearance usually matches the seafloor. They spend most of their time lying still, half buried in the sand—they sometimes only move with the tide! This all helps to hide them from predators, like sharks.

Stingrays use their hard, rounded teeth to crush the shells of bottom-dwelling animals including clams and crabs.

Jumbo stingray!

The largest known freshwater giant stingray was caught in Thailand in 2009. Unfortunately, its tail was missing—with a tail, its total length would have been around 16½ ft (5 m), and its weight, the equivalent of about ten labrador retrievers!

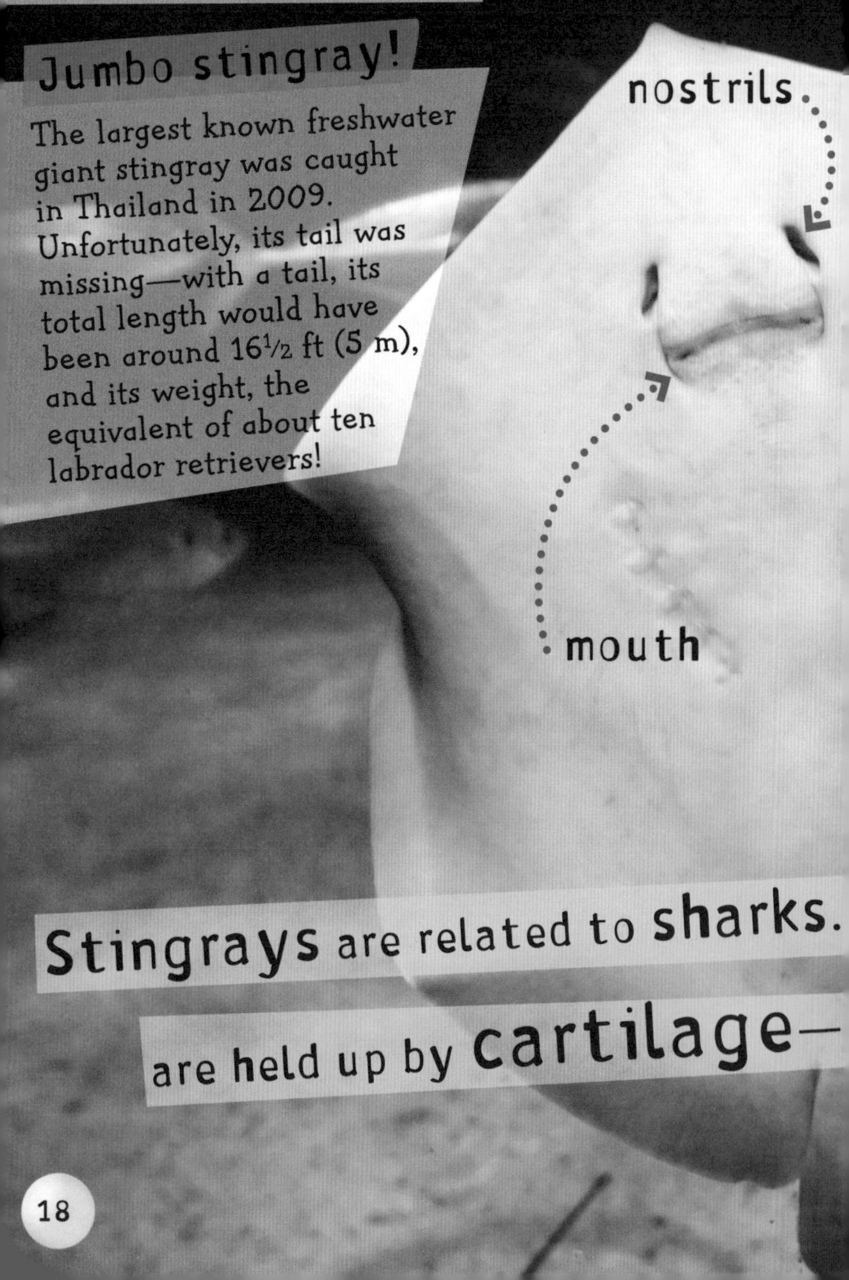

nostrils

mouth

Stingrays are related to **sharks.**

are held up by **cartilage**—

When stingrays swim, they do so by moving their body like a wave, or flapping their sides like wings!

Flapping its "wings"

Instead of bones, their bodies

the same material found

in the end of your nose!

Sweet and sour

If you're in Singapore or Malaysia, you might put some stingray on the grill and serve it with a spicy sauce. While in Iceland on December 23rd, you can join in the festive tradition of eating pickled stingray. Merry Christmas!

Dentists in Ancient Greece used the **poison** from the stingray's spine to **kill the pain** (not the patient) before treatment.

Spine

Ve-ray useful

The skin of the ray is hard and rough and has many uses. The Japanese wrap it around sword handles to give a good grip!

20

Quick Smarts

Class: *Chondrichthyes*

Family: *Dasyatidae*

Size: Apart from the giant stingray, stingrays are usually no bigger than 6½ ft (2 m) in length—that's the height of a very tall man!

Lifespan: 15–25 years in the wild.

Habitat: Stingrays are often found half buried in sand at the bottom of the seabed. They usually live in warm, tropical, saltwater.

Weapons: A sharp spine or barb in the tail, with jagged edges and a poisonous underside.

Conservation: There are currently six endangered species of stingray.

Q: Why should you have a stingray at your party?

A: Because he can always "raise" a laugh!

The hammerhead shark

With their hammer-shaped heads, and razor-sharp teeth, these are some of the fiercest—and weirdest—creatures in the sea!

Whopping winghead!

Of all the hammerheads, the winghead shark has the widest head: it can be up to half the length of its body! If adult humans were like that, our heads would be about 3 ft (1 m) wide!

fin

22

eye

hammer-shaped
head

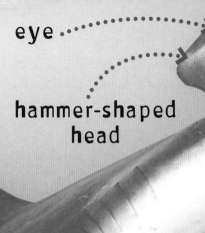

mouth

Did you know?

The hammerheads'
sense of smell is over
ten times better than
that of other sharks!
Hammerheads can
sense which direction
a smell is coming from,
making it easier to
track down prey.

Shark ahead!

Hammerhead sharks get their name from their flat,
hammer-shaped heads. Their eyes and nostrils are
at each side of the hammer, and the head itself is
called a "cephalofoil." No one really knows why
their heads are shaped this way. It probably helps
their vision and gives them a better sense of smell.
It certainly doesn't improve their looks!

Mega family

Unlike most fish, hammerheads don't lay eggs, but give birth to live young, or "pups." One pregnant female was found to be carrying 55 babies!

Great and small

There are nine known species of hammerhead sharks. The biggest is the great hammerhead, which can reach 20 ft (6 m) long and weigh up to 1,000 lb (450 kg). The smallest are the bonnetheads—but even they can reach 5 ft (1.5 m) long.

Tan-tastic!

Hammerheads are the only aquatic animals that can get sunburned! If they spend too much time in shallow waters, or close to the surface, they can get a suntan. Would you put sunblock on one? No, me neither!

Despite their **massive** heads, hammerhead sharks have very small mouths!

Hooray for stingray!

Hammerheads' favorite food is stingray. Using their wide heads they pin the stingray to the seafloor and then eat it. They don't seem to mind the deadly stings: one hammerhead was found with nearly 100 spines sticking into its mouth and throat!

Stingray

I know you're there . . .

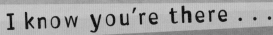

Like all sharks, hammerheads can sense tiny electrical pulses being given off by their prey. This means they can tell if their prey is there, even if it is hidden. It's like having a metal detector in your head!

Quick Smarts

Class: *Chondrichthyes*

Family: *Sphyrnidae*

Size: Bonnetheads are the smallest at 3–5 ft (1–1.5 m) long. The great hammerhead can grow from 13–20 ft (4–6 m) and weigh between 500–1,000 lb (230–450 kg).

Lifespan: In the wild, hammerheads can live for 20–30 years.

Habitat: Hammerheads are found in warmer waters and coastal waters.
They like the shallows and are sometimes found in water less than 3 ft (1 m) deep.

Weapons: Acute sense of smell, razor-sharp teeth and that weird head.

Conservation: Most hammerheads are not endangered, but they are often hunted for sport, or for their skin, which is used like leather. The great hammerhead *is* in danger, because its large fins are eaten by people in the Far East.

Q: Why did the shark cross the great barrier reef?

A: To get to the other TIDE!

Jellyfish

Jellyfish are not really fish! They are transparent, soft-bodied animals that move like a wobbly umbrella slowly opening and shutting.

Jellyfish breathe through their skin because they don't have lungs—or noses!

Jelly cannibals

Jellyfish feed on small fish and zooplankton, which get caught in their tentacles. They also eat small animals, such as shrimp—and other kinds of jellyfish! Ugh!

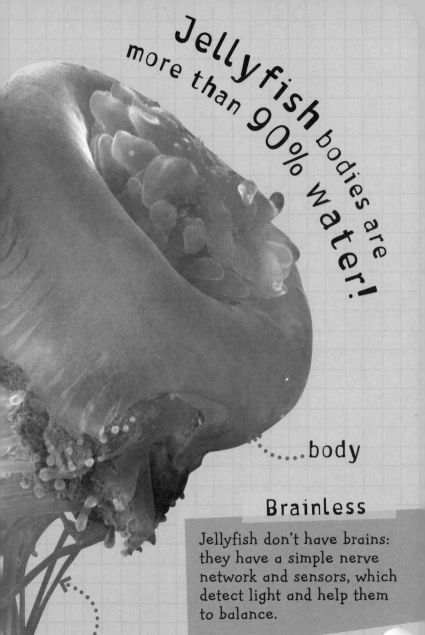

Jellyfish bodies are more than 90% water!

body

Brainless

Jellyfish don't have brains: they have a simple nerve network and sensors, which detect light and help them to balance.

tentacle

One way only!

The jellyfish's mouth is also its bottom! What goes in must come out—and quick—otherwise the jellyfish gets too heavy and starts sinking!

Toxic jellies

The box jellyfish has three million stinging cells for every 3/8 in (1 cm) of its tentacles! A sting from this jellyfish causes excruciating pain and can kill a human. But some turtles are actually immune to the stings and eat box jellies!

A jelly journey

A jellyfish starts its life as a tiny, flat creature called a "planula." The planula floats away, and sticks to the sea bottom or to a boat. It then grows into a "polyp," which looks a bit like a small stalk with feeding tentacles—its mouth and tentacles face upwards!

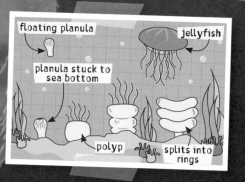

floating planula

jellyfish

planula stuck to sea bottom

polyp

splits into rings

Ring the bell!

It can be several years before the polyp changes! In the next stage, its stalk splits into rings. Each ring pulls away and becomes bell-shaped, with tentacles hanging off the bottom. These bell-shaped creatures then grow into jellyfish. Finally!

Moon jelly madness!

Jellyfish gather together in groups called blooms or swarms. Blooms can include up to 100,000 jellyfish! In the Gulf of Mexico, moon jellies have formed a huge kind of squishy net that stretches from end to end across the Gulf!

Moon jellyfish

Jellypets

Experienced people do keep jellyfish in their aquariums. (Don't try this at home though!) But irukandji jellyfish are so fragile that they cannot be kept in a normal fish tank: if they were to hit the side, it would kill them.

Quick Smarts

Class: Scyphozoa, Cubozoa, Staurozoa and some Hydrozoa

Family: Too many to mention!

Size: The lion's mane jellyfish can be more than 7 ft (2 m) wide, with tentacles up to 120 ft (36.5 m) long! The smallest jellyfish are no larger than an adult's little fingernail.

Lifespan: From a few hours to a few years. One unusual species is thought to live up to 30 years.

Habitat: Jellyfish can be found in the oceans.

Weapons: All jellyfish have tentacles with stinging cells to catch prey. Some can also be highly toxic, for example, the lion's mane jellyfish, some box jellyfish, and the irukandji jellyfish.

Conservation: Some species of jellyfish are classified as endangered, but many species reproduce at a staggering rate!

Q: How do jellyfish spend their evenings?

A: Watching jellyvision!

The killer whale

Killer whales are not whales, and they don't kill people! They are actually dolphins (also known as orcas), and the largest of their kind!

Their **teeth** can be 4 in (10 cm) long—great

for biting into

marine mammals

like **seals!**

Black is back

You can't miss killer whales with their black backs and white bellies! In the 18th century, Spanish sailors saw them killing grey whales, which is why people think they were named "killer whales."

34

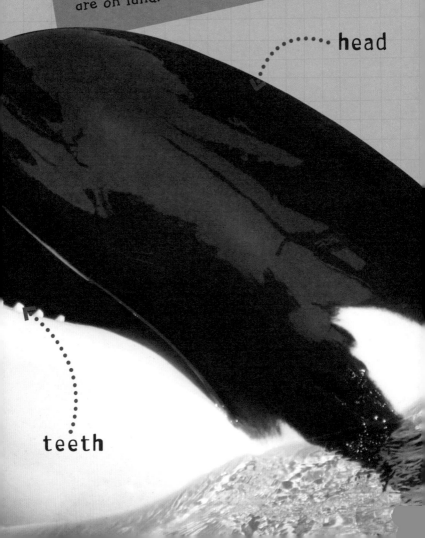

Ocean lord

Killers are one of the world's most powerful predators—but they don't eat humans. In the ocean they are at the top of the food chain, as lions and tigers are on land.

head

teeth

Powerful pods

Killer whales are very social mammals. They hunt in family groups called pods; like a pack of wolves, they work together to hunt seals, squid, and penguins, as well as other whales, dolphins, and porpoises. In all pods, the females are in charge!

The killer whale's dorsal fin is 6 ft (1.8 m) long— that's the height of a man!

dorsal fin ....

Killer whales are some of the **fastest** animals in the sea. One male reached a speed of 34.5 mph (55 kph)!

Did you know?

The killer whale has one of the biggest brains! It is four times the weight of a human brain.

Brain

Killer noise!

Killer whales scream, moan, click, and whistle to communicate. Each pod has a unique set of sounds that are recognizable from far away.

Echolocation

Killer whales also make sounds to "echolocate" their prey: the sounds travel underwater and bounce back to the killer when they hit an object. This shows the size, shape, and location of the object to the killer.

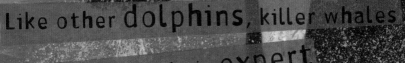

Like other **dolphins**, killer whales are known for their expert acrobatic skills!

Big eaters!

Of all the whales and dolphins, killers will tackle the largest prey. They are known to prey on other whales and dolphins, even if their prey is much larger than they are!

Quick Smarts

Class: Mammalia   **Family:** Delphinidae

Size: The average adult male is about 23–26 ft (7–8 m) long, although the longest male was measured at 32 ft (9.8 m). Killer whales can weigh up to 12,000 lb (5,440 kg).

Lifespan: In the wild, male killers live for about 35 years on average, but can reach 60 years. Females can live for about 50 years, with some living up to 80 years or more.

Habitat: Although they prefer cooler waters, killer whales are found in all oceans and most seas.

Weapons: Large size; extremely fast and strong; and they have no natural enemies as adults.

Conservation: Fewer than 100,000 worldwide, but they are not currently thought of as endangered. Used to be killed for meat and oil, but since the 1980s, they have not been hunted commercially.

Q: What do deaf killer whales wear?

A: A herring-aid!

Squids

The peculiar looking squids have been swimming around in the oceans of the world for over 100 million years.

Soft, strong, and very long

Squids belong to a group of animals called molluscs. They have eight short arms, two longer tentacles for grabbing prey, and a beak in their mouths. What looks like a large head is actually their body, which is in a bag called a "mantle."

arm

Did you know?

Squids can change color quicker than a chameleon! This helps them to "disappear" into their surroundings.

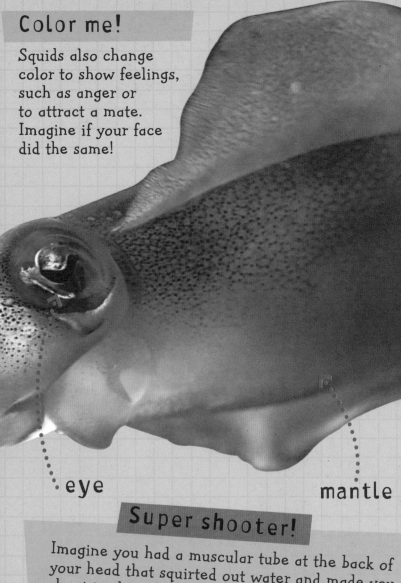

Color me!

Squids also change color to show feelings, such as anger or to attract a mate. Imagine if your face did the same!

eye

mantle

Super shooter!

Imagine you had a muscular tube at the back of your head that squirted out water and made you shoot in the other direction! That's how a squid moves. The tube is called a "siphon" and can be swivelled like a rudder on a boat to steer through the water.

Spot the difference . . .

Octopus or squid?

Octopuses have eight tentacles with suckers on them. Squids do too, but they also have those two extra tentacles to reach out and capture prey. Octopuses live in dens on the seafloor. Squids don't have dens: they live in open water.

Squids have blue blood and 3 hearts!

Who is bigger?

The largest known octopus measured 31½ ft (9.6 m) with its arms stretched out. But the longest squid is thought to be an Atlantic giant squid, measuring 55 ft 2 in (16.8 m) long—that's over ten times as long as you!

Some molluscs have no head or brain, but squids have large brains and are very clever!

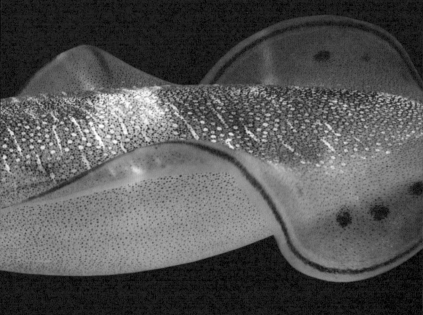

Glowing squid

The Hawaiian bobtail squid has a kind of spotlight in its belly, which is powered by glowing bacteria! It helps it find food and also masks its shadow on the seafloor so that predators are less likely to notice it. Clever!

Pen it

Most molluscs are protected by a hard outside shell, but squids have a small inside shell called a "pen."

Vampire squid

The vampire squid has a black body, eyes that can appear red, and webbed arms that look a bit like Dracula's cape! Creepy!

Eye

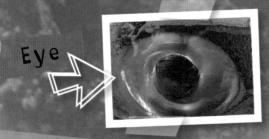

Will you look at that!

In February 2007, a New Zealand fishing vessel caught a colossal squid off the coast of Antarctica. It weighed 1,091 lb (495 kg) and measured around 33 ft (10 m) in length. It is thought that this species has the largest eyes in the animal kingdom!

Quick Smarts

Class: *Cephalopoda*

Family: *Teuthida*, which includes 29 families with around 300 different species.

Size: The longest squids are the Atlantic giant squids. They are over 750 times longer than the smallest squids, which grow to less than 1 in (2.2 cm) long!

Lifespan: Squids don't live long, possibly less than 2½ years.

Habitat: They live in saltwater and can be found in all oceans.

Weapons: Black ink! When threatened by predators, squids create a smoke-screen by squirting a cloud of ink. It acts as a warning to others, too.

Conservation: Squids are not an endangered species, but efforts are being made to protect their habitat and keep it free from pollution.

Q: Who is the most dangerous squid in the sea?

A: Billy the Squid!

45

The whale shark

This monster is the largest fish in the sea. It can grow up to 41½ ft (12.65 m) in length— that's as big as a bus!

The whale shark's skin can be up to 4 in (10 cm) thick.

mouth

Massive mouth!

A whale shark's mouth can open as wide as 5 ft (1.5 m)—it could swallow you whole! (Don't worry, they only eat plankton, microscopic plants, and small fish.)

Fish or whale?

The whale shark is a fish, not a whale. A whale is a mammal and breathes air with its lungs. A fish gets oxygen from the water passing over its gills.

Fishy stories

There are stories of whale sharks between 50 and 65 ft (15–20 m) long, but none of these monsters have ever been caught. They're probably just scary stories!

The **biggest** whale shark ever caught weighed more than 47,300 lb (21,450 kg)!

A whale of a shark

The whale shark gets its name because of its size and also because it feeds like a whale. It sucks in a mouthful of water, closes its mouth, then squirts the water out through its gills. Anything left behind is dinner!

Whale sharks are quite friendly towards divers—the only risk is being hit accidentally by that huge tail!

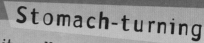

Stomach-turning

If it swallows anything too big, the whale shark can turn its stomach inside out and spit the contents back out through its mouth. It's called "gastric eversion." Yuck!

Did you know?

Whale sharks can suck in about 1,320 gallons (6,000 litres) of seawater each hour. That's like drinking nearly 17,000 cans of soda!

Unique ID

Each whale shark has a different pattern of spots on its skin. Like our fingerprints, a whale shark can be identified by these spots. Scientists can use computers to spot individual sharks, using software originally created to identify stars and galaxies!

Whale sharks can dive down over 2,300 ft (700 m)!

Star spotting

The Kenyan name for a whale shark is "*papa shillingi*." This comes from a story where God threw shillings (old coins) onto the shark, which then turned into its spots. In Madagascar, whale sharks are known as "*marokintana*," which means "lots of stars."

Quick Smarts

Class: *Chondrichthyes*

Family: *Rhincodontidae*

Size: Whale sharks measure up to 41 1/2 ft (12.65 m) in length and weigh up to 47,300 lb (21,450 kg).

Lifespan: No one is sure. Estimates vary between 50 and 100 years!

Habitat: Whale sharks are found in tropical and warm oceans.

Weapons As the biggest fish in the sea, their only real enemy is man.

Conservation: Their large size, slow speed and friendly behavior makes them easy prey for hunters. Populations are declining, and they are a threatened species.

Q: What does a whale shark sing at Christmas?

A: Shark the herald angels sing!

The anglerfish

These are some of the strangest fish in the sea. Some anglerfish live nearer the surface, but most live deep down in the darkest depths!

Come and get it!

Anglerfish get their name from the "fishing rod" that hangs in front of their mouths. Deep-sea anglerfish live in complete darkness, so their rods light up. When other fish see it waving, they think it's a little fish, come to take the bait and GULP!

teeth

52

Anglerfish are some of the **ugliest** fish on the planet!

tail

Big belly

Anglerfish can swallow prey up to twice their own size! Their bodies can expand to the size of their prey.

No escape!

Anglerfish have huge heads and massive mouths lined with sharp teeth. Their ferocious teeth are angled inwards so that their prey cannot escape.

Anglerfish can be up to 3 ft (1 m) long. Most are much smaller—often less than 5 in (12 cm)—which is about the length of a pen!

Wobblers

Due to their wide, round bodies, most deep-sea anglerfish can't swim fast. Instead, they wobble slowly through the water.

Anglerfish have transparent teeth! Weird!

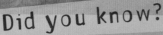

Did you know?

An anglerfish from the species *Photocorynus spiniceps* is the smallest vertebrate fish in the world. Scientists found a female who was just over 1¾ in (46 mm) long, and attached to her back was a male that was less than ¼ in (6.2 mm) long!

Fatal attraction!

When a young male angler meets a female, he bites her, releasing a substance that melts the skin around his mouth and "glues" him to her body. After that, he loses his eyes and all his internal organs to become a permanent part of her body!

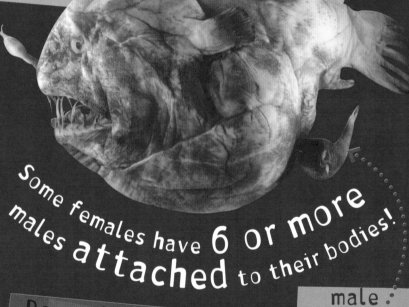

Some females have **6 or more** males **attached** to their bodies!

male: anglerfish

Deep, deep down

Deep-sea anglerfish live deep down in the ocean. They are found in dark and freezing water at depths of over 3,300 ft (1,000 m)— that's as much as ten Statues of Liberty!

Quick Smarts

Class: *Actinopterygii*

Family: Various

Size: From 3 ft (1 m) to a very tiny ¼ in (6.2 mm)!

Lifespan: It varies, but some anglerfish can live for 25 or 30 years.

Habitat: Found throughout the world's oceans. Some live in the harshest, deepest, darkest, and coldest seas.

Weapons The fishing rod lure; those huge sharp teeth; and they can swallow fish up to twice their own size!

Conservation: They are not endangered as far as we know. But they live in such remote places, it's hard to tell.

Q: What do anglerfish get when they finish school?

A: A deep-loma!

57

The blue whale

The blue whale is not just the largest animal around today, it's the largest animal that has ever existed. Now that really is a monster!

Don't drink the water!

Whales don't drink! Despite being surrounded by water, they can't drink seawater. Experts think that they get all the water they need from the food they eat.

Colossal calves

When they are born, blue whale calves weigh the same as an adult hippopotamus!

Hippo

A blue whale can grow up to 108 ft (33 m) in length—that's longer than a basketball court!

Did you know?

This massive monster actually eats some of the tiniest animals in the sea. It mainly eats krill, which are little shrimplike creatures.

In for the krill!

Blue whales normally feed at a depth of around 330 ft (100 m). They lunge forward and take in a huge mouthful of seawater. Then they squeeze the water out and catch any krill, small fish, or squids. When fully open, their mouths can hold 200,000 lb (90,700 kg) of food and water!

Blowhole

Blow your nose!

Blue whales breathe through blowholes on the top of their bodies. These holes are like a huge pair of nostrils, only they are large enough for a toddler to crawl into! When blue whales breathe out, the spray from their blowholes can shoot to the height of a three-story building!

The blue whale's throat is so small that it can't swallow anything bigger than a beach ball!

Blue whales can dive as deep as 1,640 ft (500 m).

Waxy whales

Scientists can work out the age of a blue whale by counting the layers of its wax-like earplugs— a little like counting the rings on a tree. They think the oldest blue whale was around 110 years old.

A blue whale can be louder than a jet plane, but its "song" is so low that most humans would never hear it!

Long and loud!

Blue whales are the loudest animals on the planet: they can hear each other up to 1,000 miles (1,600 km) away. That's like saying something in London and being heard at the bottom of Italy!

Quick Smarts

Class: *Mammalia*

Family: *Balaenopteridae*

Size: From 82–105 ft (25–32 m) long and with a weight of nearly 400,000 lb (up to 180,000 kg)—or 36 African elephants!

Lifespan: No one's really sure. Estimates vary between 50 and 100 years!

Habitat: The blue whale is found in all oceans. It prefers deeper water and is rarely found near the coast.

Weapons: Huge size and a massively powerful tail. They're the biggest animals ever. You want to mess with them?

Conservation: Endangered. Until whaling was banned in the 1960s, thousands of whales were killed every year. Scientists think there are under 5,000 left, although the numbers are growing.

Q: Where do you weigh a blue whale?

A: At a whale-weigh station!

Index